David Jumps In

Written by
Alan Woo

Illustrated by
Katty Maurey

KIDS CAN PRESS

It was David's first day
At his brand-new school.

He didn't know anyone.
He had no friends
To hang out with
Or trade tuna fish sandwiches.

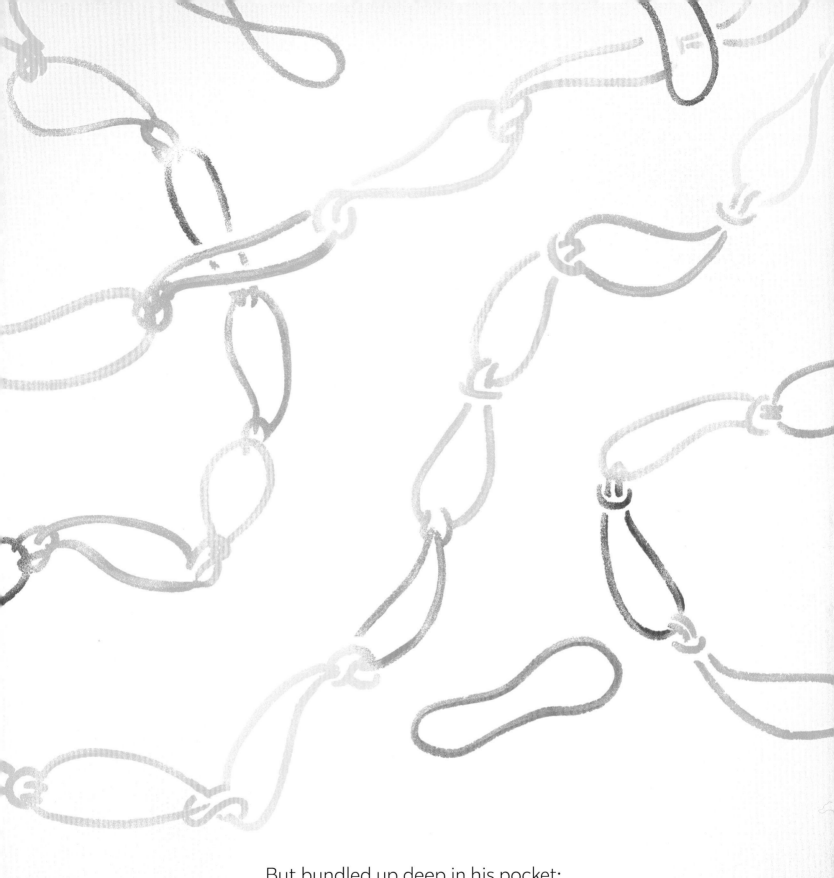

But bundled up deep in his pocket:
A string of rubber bands
Knotted and ready
For a game of elastic skip.
But who else would want to play that?
He wondered.

When the recess bell rang,
The kids raced into sunshine,
Clamoring for first place
At the swings, slides
And monkey bars.

Hand in hand they went ring-around-the-rosy,
Linked arms in red-rover rows
That wanted YOU to come over,
Or hiding and seeking
With shouts of "Ready or not, here I come!"

Others practiced
Their California kicks,
Sending soccer balls flying
Through invisible nets.

Some sat on the sidelines,
Blowing dandelions into
A galaxy of stars.

"Tag, you're it!" an older boy hollered,
Chasing after his friend
And winding up tangled
In a double Dutch sing–along
Of bluebells, cockleshells,
Eevy, ivy, over.

"Do you want to play?" David asked around.
But the video-game kids
Didn't hear him —
Didn't even look up.

The bookworms —
Off on faraway adventures ...

David looked around nervously.
What if nobody wanted to play with him?

He spotted a few classmates
Tired of hopscotching
Back and forth
And forth and back —
A one-foot balancing act —
Throwing stones to land
Inside chalk-drawn squares.

Taking a deep breath, he stepped toward them.
"Hey," he said shyly. "I'm David.
Do you want to play elastic skip?"

"How do you play?" asked a friendly redheaded girl.

David explained

The jumping

And the chanting

And the rubber bands.

From his pocket he pulled
His chain-link rainbow of
Red
Blue
Green
And yellow
To create a new playing field
Where they stomped the ground
With both feet,
Jumping in and out,
Shouting "2, 4, 6, 8 …"

The next day at school,
When the recess bell rang,
David and his newfound friends
Raced into sunshine
For a chance to be champions
In a world of their own.

This book is dedicated to library people everywhere! — A.W.
For little Jessie June — K.M.

Author's Note:

The game David plays in this story has its origins in ancient China. Here I've called it "elastic skip," but the game is known by many different names around the world, including Chinese Jump Rope, Elastics, Jumpsies, French Skipping, American or Chinese Ropes — or Chinese Skip, as I used to call it. What is it called where you live? If you'd like to learn how to play, you'll find many resources online; ask a grown-up to help you search — they might even remember playing when they were a kid!

Text © 2020 Alan Woo
Illustrations © 2020 Katty Maurey

Kids Can Press gratefully acknowledges the financial support of the Government of Ontario, through Ontario Creates; the Ontario Arts Council; the Canada Council for the Arts; and the Government of Canada for our publishing activity.

Published in Canada and the U.S. by Kids Can Press Ltd.
25 Dockside Drive, Toronto, ON M5A 0B5

Kids Can Press is a Corus Entertainment Inc. company

www.kidscanpress.com

The artwork in this book was rendered digitally.
The text is set in Karu.

Edited by Yvette Ghione
Designed by Karen Powers

Printed and bound in Shenzhen, China, in 10/2019 by C & C Offset

CM 20 0 9 8 7 6 5 4 3 2 1

Library and Archives Canada Cataloguing in Publication

Title: David jumps in / written by Alan Woo ; illustrated by Katty Maurey.

Names: Woo, Alan, 1977– author. | Maurey, Katty, illustrator.

Identifiers: Canadiana 20190170867 | ISBN 9781771388450 (hardcover)

Subjects: LCGFT: Fiction.

Classification: LCC PS8645.O47 D38 2020 | DDC jC813/.6—dc23